PIGGYBOOK

Anthony Browne

Dragonfly Books New York

 Published in the United States by Dragonfly Books, an imprint of Random House Children's Books, a division of Random House, Inc., New York. Originally published in hardcover in Great Britain by Julia MacRae Books, a division of Walker Books Limited, London, and in the United States by Alfred A. Knopf Books for Young Readers, an imprint of Random House Children's Books, a division of Random House, Inc., New York, in 1986.

Visit us on the Web! www.randomhouse.com/kids

Educators and librarians, for a variety of teaching tools, visit us at
www.randomhouse.com/teachers

Library of Congress Cataloging-in-Publication Data
Browne, Anthony.
Piggybook.
Summary: When Mrs. Piggott unexpectedly leaves one day, her demanding family begins to realize just how much she did for them.
ISBN 978-0-394-88416-5 (trade) — ISBN 978-0-394-98416-2 (lib. bdg.) —
ISBN 978-0-679-80837-4 (pbk.)
[1. Mothers—Fiction. 2. Family life—Fiction.] I. Title.
PZ7.B81984Pi 1986 [E] 86003008

MANUFACTURED IN CHINA
27 26 25 24 23 22 21

For Julia

Mr. Piggott lived with his two sons, Simon and Patrick, in a nice house with a nice garden, and a nice car in the nice garage.
Inside the house was his wife.

"Hurry up with the breakfast, dear," he called every morning before he went off to his very important job.

"Hurry up with the breakfast, Mom," Simon and Patrick called before they went off to their very important school.

After they left the house, Mrs. Piggott washed all the breakfast things,

made all the beds,

vacuumed all the carpets,

and then went to work.

"Hurry up with the meal, Mom," the boys called every evening when they came home from their very important school.

"Hurry up with the meal, old girl," Mr. Piggott called every evening when he came home from his very important job.

As soon as they had eaten,
Mrs. Piggott washed the dishes,

washed the clothes,

did the ironing,

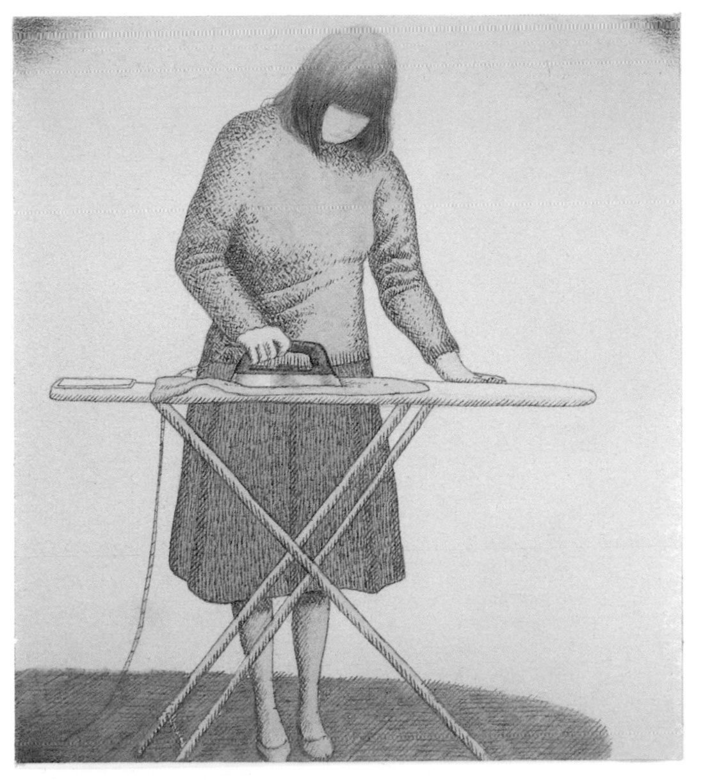

and then cooked some more.

One evening when the boys got home from school, there was no one to greet them.

“Where’s Mom?” demanded Mr. Piggott when he got home from work.

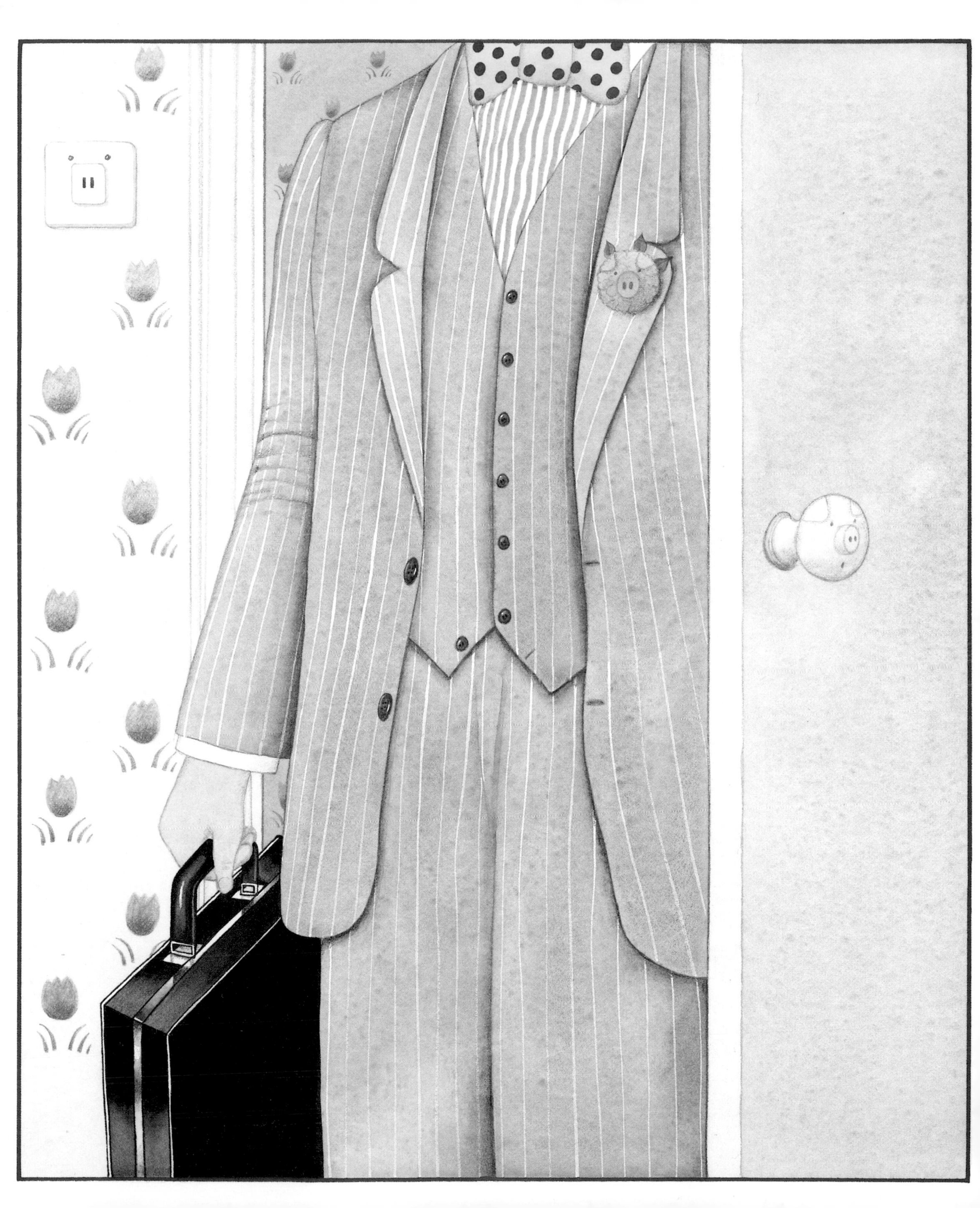

She was nowhere to be found.
On the mantelpiece was an envelope.
Mr. Piggott opened it.
Inside was a piece of paper.

"But what shall we *do*?" said Mr. Piggott.
They had to make their own meal.
It took hours.
And it was horrible.

The next morning they had to make their own breakfast.
It took hours.
And it was horrible.

The next day and the next night and the day after that, Mrs. Piggott was still not there. Mr. Piggott, Simon, and Patrick tried to take care of themselves.
They never washed the dishes. They never washed their clothes. Soon the house was like a pigsty.

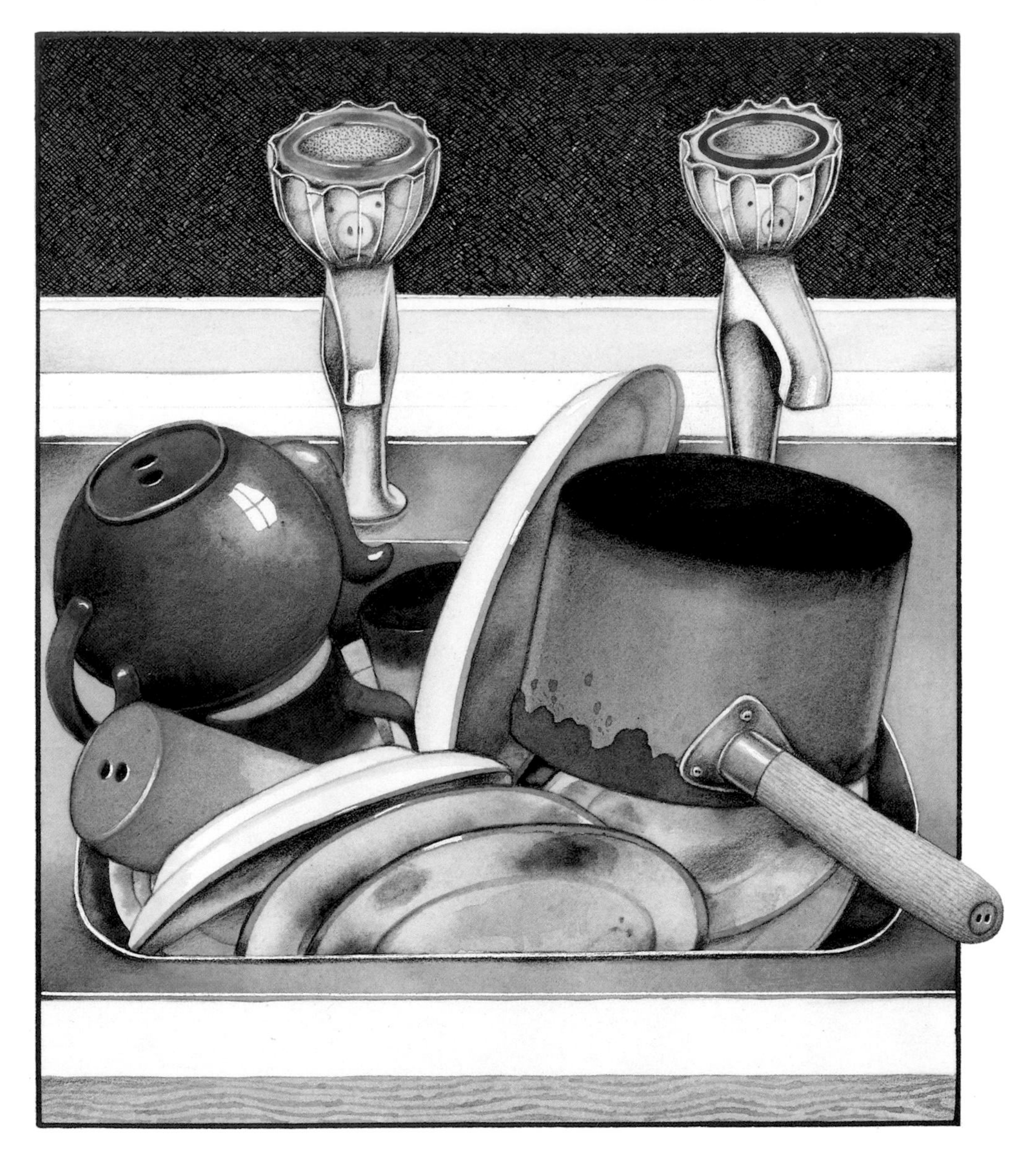

"When is Mom coming home?" the boys squealed after another horrible meal.
"How should I know?" Mr. Piggott grunted.
They all became more and more grumpy.

One night there was nothing in the house for them to cook. "We'll just have to root around and find some scraps," snorted Mr. Piggott.

And just then Mrs. Piggott walked in.

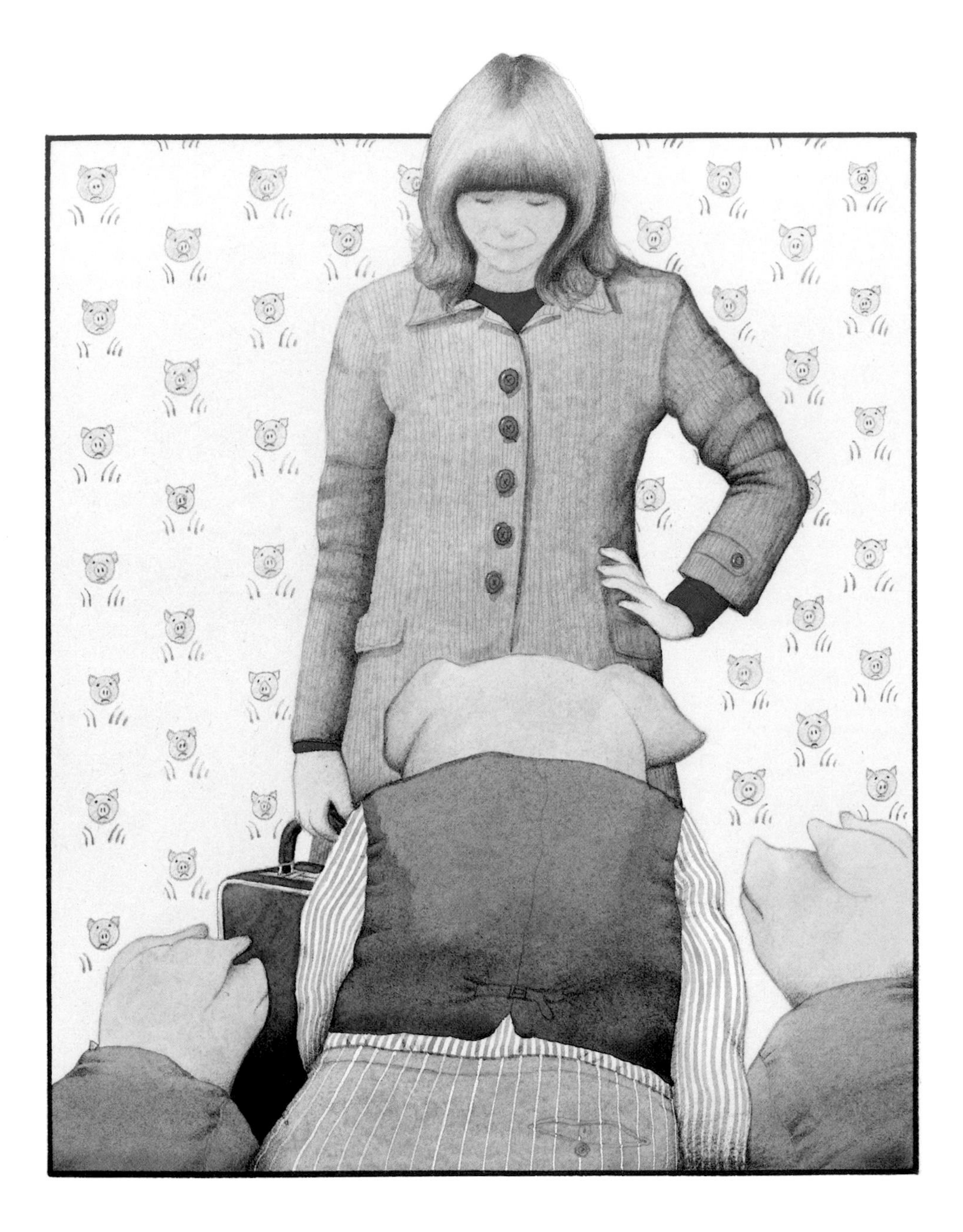

"P-L-E-A-S-E come back," they snuffled.

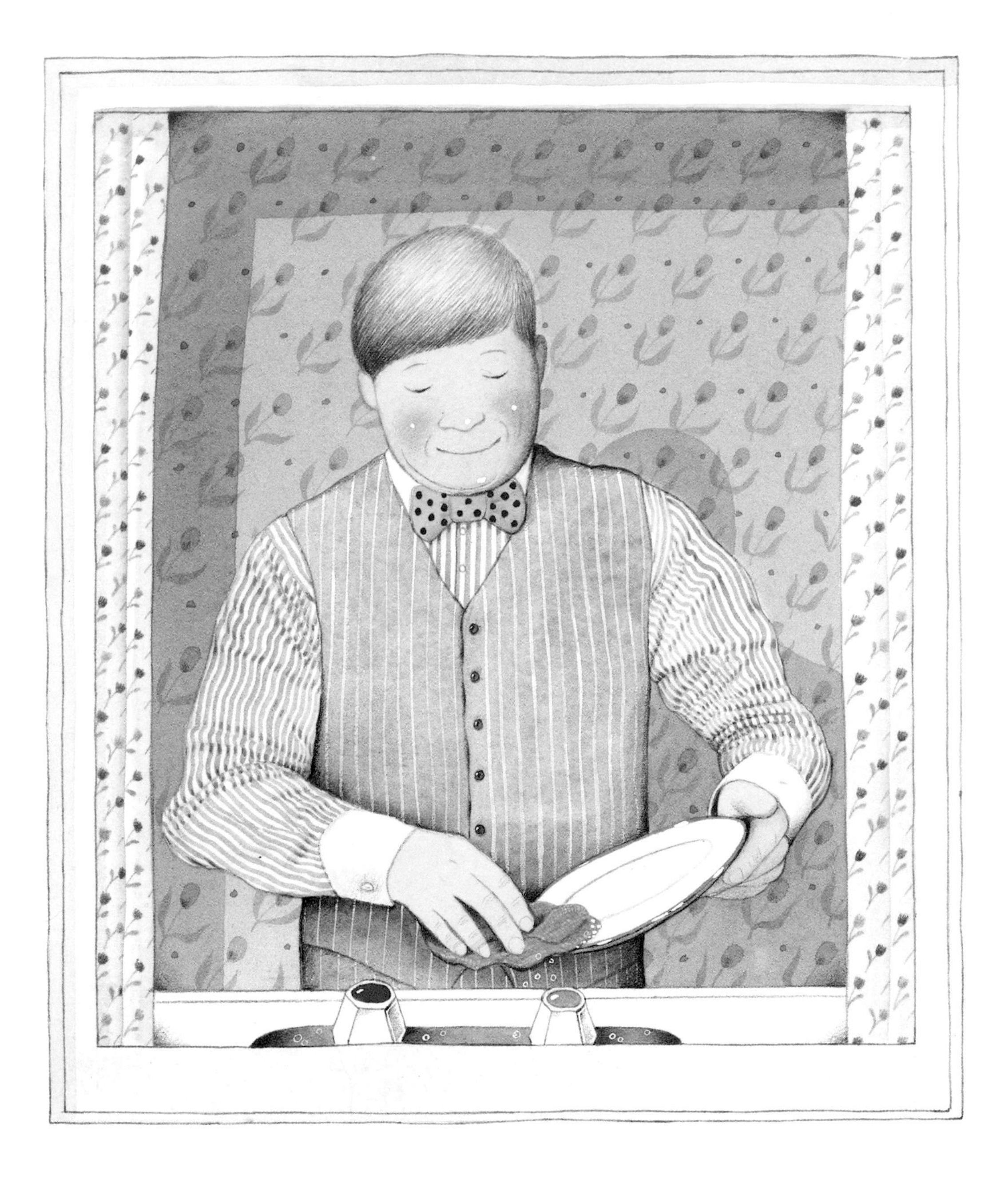

So Mrs. Piggott stayed.
Mr. Piggott washed the dishes.

Patrick and Simon made the beds.

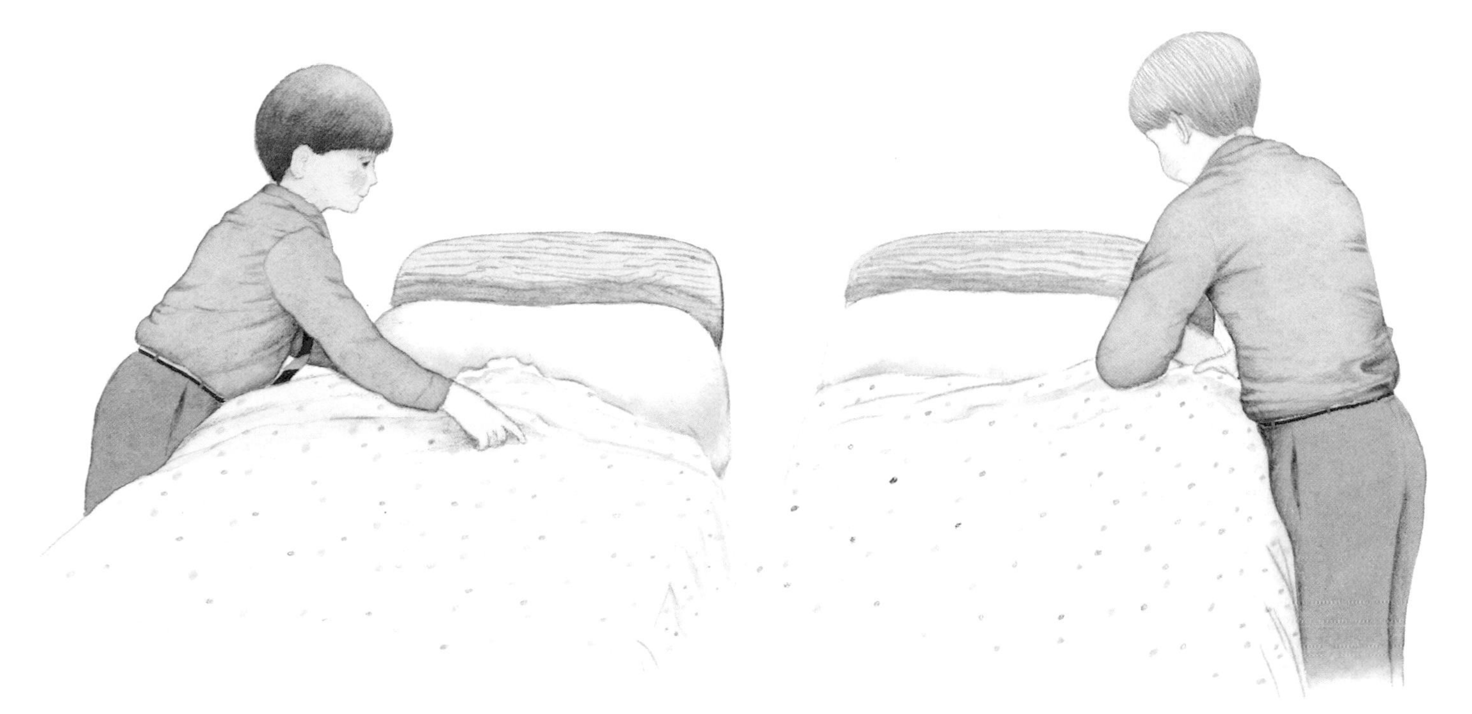

Mr. Piggott did the ironing.

And they all helped with the cooking.
Sometimes they even sort of liked it.

Mom was happy too.

She fixed the car.